HOME PRACTICE MANUAL

Based on principles found in Ashtanga yoga, somatic and developmental movement, experiential anatomy, acro-yoga and Yin yoga

by
April Nunes Tucker PhD

The author and publisher disclaim, as far as the law allows, any liability arising directly or indirectly from the use, or misuse, of the information contained in this manual.

™ April Nunes Tucker 2016
Text copyright © April Nunes Tucker 2016
Photography by Carli Spokes 2016
http://createdbycarli.bigcartel.com

All rights reserved

Models: April Nunes Tucker, Lincoln Tucker and Grace Tucker

This manual is best used in conjunction with the teachings presented in a Big Dog Little Dog class as offered by a qualified Big Dog Little Dog teacher (see www.bdld.co.uk). Additionally, it is to be enjoyed by adult yoga enthusiasts with children aged 4-8 as part of a home practice. This manual is sold subject to the condition that it shall not, by way of trade and otherwise, be lent, resold, hired out, or otherwise circulated without the publisher's prior consent in any form or binding or cover other than that in which it is published and without a similar condition being imposed on the subsequent purchaser.

In any physical activity, risk of serious physical injury is possible. Yoga is no substitute for medical diagnosis and treatment. Big Dog Little Dog yoga and/or specific yoga poses are not recommended for individuals with certain conditions (e.g., cardiac illness, later stages of pregnancy, herniated disks, post-surgery etc.) with this knowledge, the purchaser of this manual assumes the risk of the yoga practice and releases Big Dog Little Dog and its qualified teachers from any liability claims.

TABLE OF CONTENTS

Foreword

The Big Dog Little Dog Home Practice

1) **CONNECT**
    Breath

2) **WARM**
    Mirroring/Partnering Yoga Poses
        Cat/Cow/Dog
        Child's pose to all fours series
        Double Plank
        Double Down Dog
        Dolphin
        See-Saw Balance
    The Developmental Movement Sequence
        Starfish Breathing
        Caterpillar
        Frog and Donkey
        Lizard
        Cat
        Bear
    The Power of Image

3) **FLY**
    Preparing to Fly
        Leg Press
    The Flying Poses, Mounts and Dismounts
        Forward Fly
        Deep Fold
        The Thinker
        Hedgehog
        Revolving Hedgehog
        Kick-over Dismount
        Overhead Mount

Angel
Backward Fly
Reverse Bow
Rag Doll
The Hanger
Cuddle Dismount
Stirrup Mount
High Chair

4) **SUPPORT**
Headstand
Handstand
Shoulderstand

5) **CALM**
Leg Love
The Washing Machine
Kissing Twist
Soft Folds

6) **REST**

About the author

Bibliography

Foreword

The Big Dog Little Dog curriculum has developed organically over the years. I taught my first Big Dog Little Dog class in 2013 when my son was just four years old. It was an opportunity for us to do yoga together. When my daughter turned three she started coming to the Big Dog Little Dog classes too – and my husband would come along. I would teach the class (usually demonstrating with my son Lincoln) and my husband Iain would work with Grace (my daughter). The class has risen in popularity over the years and it feels right to train more teachers so that this unique sharing of yoga can continue on a more widely spread basis. My vision for the Big Dog Little Dog classes is to bring parents/carers and their children together through a shared experience of yoga.

In our world of screens and mobile devices, which easily separate us from one another, human contact and commitment to *be-ing* are more necessary than ever. When my children were toddlers, every class they attended: Gymboree, Little Kickers, Music Together, Busy Babes...I attended with them. I sang all the silly songs, played the finger cymbals, chased a baby-sized football around a massive gymnasium... Then, when they turned four, I was expected to leave them and become the taxi-ing service. This correlated to them starting school and the separation from them seemed quite stark. I am an advocate of a child's independence but I do believe (although it sounds cliché) that the quality of time you spend with your child is possibly more important than the quantity.

Big Dog Little Dog is a rebel yell to handing your child your mobile phone instead of holding them, to placing them in front of the TV instead of engaging with them, to dropping them off at [insert any name] classes. My children do watch (some) TV and I do take them to swim lessons...but this is not a parenting manual.

The point of Big Dog Little Dog is to build connection and trust between children and their parents/carers for 45 minutes, once a week. It may not sound like much but I believe that in a Big Dog Little Dog practice children and their parents/carers can learn to build trust between one another, they can express the love that they have for one another and they can experience a sense of play together. This is healthy. This is all in the form of yoga-based principles. Things I know to be true and why I believe Big Dog Little Dog works as a bonding tool is:

1) Children love undivided attention from their parents/carers because they experience it rarely.

2) An adult/child relationship where support is mutual is unique; children love feeling needed.

3) We all breathe – what a wonder it is to have time focused on just breathing with your child.

4) Human touch is vital for our well-being; without it we suffer.

5) Yoga brings a sense of calm through the experience of focused breath and movement.

6) People's lives are busy and rushed. If we don't slow down and engage with it, it will pass by.

7) People have a desire to be healthy; yoga promotes health.

8) Parents often feel guilty about the quality of the relationship they have with their children. Big Dog Little Dog nurtures this relationship.

9) Playing is fun! Kids love being upside down, using their bodies to express themselves and how much more fun to do it with someone that loves them.

The Big Dog Little Dog practice has six components: CONNECT, WARM, FLY, SUPPORT, CALM and REST. CONNECT is the first and establishes focus for what is to come. Although don't feel bound to follow these sections through from start to finish. It may be enough to simply spend five minutes from any section on any given day.

CONNECT

THE BREATH:
This opening section of the Big Dog Little Dog practice connects you and your child through the most basic function of our existence: our breath.

> ...simply let yourself breathe. There is peace in just letting your body breathe, without having to do anything about it. Imagine letting your hands breathe. Just let them be, without having to control them. Just let them breathe. Now look around you and just let each thing in the room breathe. See the people around you and just let them breathe. When you let them breathe, you just let them be, exactly as they are. You don't need to change them. You don't need to control them. You don't need to improve them. Just let them breathe, in peace, and you accept that. You might even smile at this breathing. As you go through your day, let everything breathe. Let yourself breathe. There is no need to do anything. You don't expect anything from anything or anybody. Let them come as they come, let them go as they go. Just appreciate everything and everybody as they are, miracles of existence, breathing in the soft air of the world, and smile at this joyful manifestation of love. (Levine)

Breathing, holding your child, feeling your child breathing. Just this. This is a good way to start. It is simple and bonding.

Let yourselves breathe together for a bit.

Some other possibilities for these first few moments of your practice could be:

· See what it feels like to match your child's breathing in terms of tempo and quality and then observe in yourself what it takes to do this.
·   Ask your child if they could try to match your breathing...what would it take for them to try and achieve this?
· Have your child place an eye bag on their abdomen and watch the eye bag rise and fall with their natural relaxed breathing. Let them know that there is no need to try to make the eye bag move. It will move on its own with soft-belly breathing. Both of you can try this. Take time to watch each other just breathe.

We're all breathing. The instruction is just to know that we are, not in an intellectual sense, but to be aware of the simple sensations, the in-breath and the out-breath. Even in this first instruction, we are learning something extremely important, to allow the breathing to follow its own nature, to breathe itself. We are not trying to make the breath deep or keep it shallow. We are seeing how it is.
(Rosenberg, 1998:20)

Soft Belly Breathing –

Taking a few deep breaths, feel the body you breathe in.
Feel the body expanding and contracting with each breath.
Focus on the rising and falling of the abdomen.
Let awareness receive the beginning, middle and end
    of each inbreath, of each outbreath
    expanding and contracting the belly.
Note the constantly changing flow of sensation in
    each inhalation, in each exhalation.
And begin to soften all around these sensations.
Let the breath breathe itself in a softening belly.
Soften the belly to receive the breath,
    to receive sensation, to experience life in the body.
Soften the muscles that have held the fear for so long.
Soften the tissue, the blood vessels, the flesh.
Letting go of the holding of a lifetime.
Letting go into soft-belly, merciful belly.
Soften the grief, the distrust, the anger
    held so hard in the belly.
Levels and levels of softening, levels and levels of letting go.
Moment to moment allow each breath its full expression
    in soft-belly.
Let go of the hardness. Let it float
    in something softer and kinder.
Let thoughts come and let them go,
    floating like bubbles in the spaciousness of soft-belly.
Holding to nothing, softening, softening.
Let the healing in.
Let the pain go.
Have mercy on yourself, soften the belly,
    open the passageway to the heart.
In soft-belly there is room to be born at last,
    and room to die when the moment comes.
In soft-belly is the vast spaciousness in which to heal,
    in which to discover our unbounded nature.
Letting go into the softness,
    fear floats in the gentle vastness we call the heart.

Soft-belly is the practice that accompanies us throughout the day and finds us at day's end still alive and well.

(Levine, S. 1997:32-33)

EXPERIENTIAL ANATOMY

Experiential anatomy is a way of feeling our anatomy from the inside – from an embodied perspective. Through experiential anatomy children are able to feel the forms and functions of their bones and muscles through touch with you. This is intimate work and work that ultimately bonds us deeper with our child. The nature of touch and types of touch is an involved area of study so as a general rule: simply touch with love.

An exploration of the musculature of the face is an easy way to start with the idea of experiential anatomy. You can begin by holding your child's head in your hands and feel the weight of their head. Let the weight of their head relax in your hands and then provide a gentle nod (yes) movement as you rock the skull gently on the Atlas (the bone at the top of the cervical spine). Feel with your fingers along the base of the Occipital bone (base of the skull) and then you can trace your fingers up and into the TMJ (Temporomandibular joint) commonly referred to as the jaw.

Follow your intuition but from here you could start to move the jaw gently (up and down and side to side) or travel up to the Temporal bones (sides of the head). Another possible pathway is to move from the back of the skull up and along the back midline of the skull until you arrive at the crown (where the sagittal and coronal sutures meet). This is a place which may still be 'soft' on some children so go gently. Feel free to move down across the Frontal bone (forehead), giving a light squeeze to the nasal bone before tracing the eyes and returning to hold the base of the skull. Then switch places (where the child holds your head – note that for a child this can feel quite heavy. An adult's skull weighs between 12-14 pounds!

Grace using gentle touch on the Frontal bone.

Still reclining or if you prefer, coming up to sitting, you can begin to explore how a release through the muscles of the head and jaw effects a decrease in tension held in the neck and shoulders. Time can be taken to explore how the Sternocloidomastoids (strong muscles in the front of the neck) tie the skull and clavicles together.

Lincoln locates the clavicles...

and the rhomboids!

The Experiential Anatomy section of your practice does not need to be daunting. It can be explored in a light-hearted way. One exercise worth doing is to work together to build a representation of the human spine and ribcage using found objects. It is fun in itself to go out and collect stones, sticks, pine cones, shells or any other found objects that you may wish to use.

This is a photograph of a four year old Big Dog Little Dog student and her daddy working on building a model of the spine. She has used a pine cone for skull, white stones for the cervical vertebrae (there are seven), red stones for the thoracic vertebra (there are 12), sticks for the ribs (there are 12), shells for the lumbar vertebra (there are 5) and a large stone for the sacrum (there is one and it is just under her hand in the photograph). Her dad has laid down so that she can see how to place the objects in relationship to the real thing.

After completing the CONNECT section of the Big Dog Little Dog practice you could move to the WARM section. From an initial focus on the breath and after building concentration and focus through Experiential Anatomy there are two ways to approach the WARM section. One way is through the Mirroring/Partnering Yoga Poses Section and the other is through the Developmental Movement Sequence.

WARM

The purpose of the WARM section in the Big Dog Little Dog practice is to continue the connection built on breath awareness and start to move the body together with your child which examine more involved developmental patterning and strength work.

> Positive and affirming interactions with others, particularly parents and teachers, assist young children in developing reasonable expectations for themselves and positive regard for their physical characteristics and abilities. Providing opportunities to enhance motor skills that are appropriate to age and capabilities facilitates individual physical and motor competence and the formulation of positive self-concepts and self-esteem.
> (Black & Puckett, 2005:428)

MIRRORING/PARTNER YOGA POSES

Coming back up to sitting after soft-belly breathing is an easy transition to then face each other and rub your own hands together to create heat between the hands.

Rub the hands quickly together until they feel "hot" and then open them up (palm towards palm) to your partner's hands. Just "feel" the heat here. Do not actually touch your hands to your partner's hands. This can be done a couple times and children really enjoy the energy building aspect of it.

A simple mirroring exercise can follow on from this – this is a nice way to work with the idea of 'feeling' each other, moving slowly and thoughtfully and fostering concentration. The 'leader' can shift between you and your child. For an extra challenge you can try the mirroring exercise with 'no leader'.

Mirroring

From here partnering yoga poses can develop. The traditional *cat/cow* done with optional *cat/cow* sound effects if a fun way to warm the spine. Sometimes we do what I call *kissing cow*. This is where you give your child a kiss every time you move into *cow* (hyper-extension of spine - where the sping 'hangs' towards the floor). You can also become a *dog* and look back at your own 'tail'. This action moves the spine into lateral flexion.

Dog looking at his own tail

Cat moves the spine into flexion.

Cow moves the spine into extension and then hyper-extension.

Some transitional partnering work to link *cat/cow* and the more energetic partnering poses which follow is the *Child's Pose to all fours series*. It starts with the you (the adult) in *child's pose* and then your child 'sits' on your back. Your child can then lay back completely, feeling supported by your body.

Stage 1 of the *Child's pose to all fours series*

Once the child feels secure then you can lift up onto all fours. Establishing trust of weight, the child can feel supported, ready for the poses in the FLY section.

Stage 2 of the *Child's pose to all fours series*

Stage 3 of the *Child's pose to all fours series*

Double plank, *double down dog* and *dolphin* are additional warming partnering yoga postures to try:

Double plank

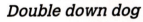
Double down dog

Dolphin

Dolphin can be done (like *down dog* but with elbows on the ground and then moving your chin in front of your hands and back again). This can be done side by side, facing each other or individually with your partner counting repetitions...
Can mum make it to 10?!

From here, and an easy introduction to the FLY section of the practice is to try the *see-saw balance*.

Let your child take their first foothold...and then their second. Allow them to continue to 'climb' up to where their feet are resting on your thighs. Once your child is steady and standing then both of you can lean back and feel the counter-weight.

From here you may feel confident enough to let go of one hand still keeping your *see-saw balance*.

After this you should be warm and ready to FLY! Alternatively, you may wish to play together working through some of the Developmental Movement Sequence.

The Developmental Movement Sequence used in the Big Dog Little Dog classes starts with the *Starfish Breathing* exercise. *Starfish Breathing* illustrates the importance of breath-movement synchronicity in yoga practice. For example, in Ashtanga yoga this breath-movement synchronicity is fundamental to the practice and is called *vinyasa* (Scott, 2000:19-20). In the Big Dog Little Dog class this breath-movement synchronicity is introduced in a playful, natural way whilst still placing emphasis on the importance on these two things (breath and movement) happening together and influencing one another.

> The radial symmetry of the starfish is an old prevertebral developmental pattern which is encoded in the body from our evolutionary heritage (Olsen, 1998:131).

Exploring the *Starfish Breathing* exercise allows you both to access age old human developmental patterns which relate to: flexion and extension of the limbs around the centre of the body as well as a bonding with gravity with the back body and a sense of navel radiation.

Starfish Breathing is a five part breath-movement exercise. The movement is done in conjunction with the exhale. During inhalation the body remains in stillness, softening in each place. It is nice to do several repetitions of *Starfish Breathing* to find the regulatory rhythm of the breath-movement cycle.

> Connection with gravity towards weight and rest and reaching into space towards lightness and activity provide a span of dynamic range and health in the body. (Olsen, 1998:135)

Starfish Breathing Part 1: **Inhaling** whilst bonding with gravity through the back of the body and experiencing the 'six limbs' (head, tail, arms and legs) in relationship to the centre (navel).

Part 2: **Exhaling** - link breath and movement to flex the limbs into the body and then stay here and **inhale**.

Part 3: **Exhale** and extend the limbs up into space. **Inhale** and relax there.

Part 4: Exhale and return the limbs to flexion in toward the centre of the body. **Inhale** and stay there.

Part 5: **Exhale** and unfurl the limbs back into gravity. **Inhale** and relax here.

Starfish Breathing can be repeated as many times as you like, remembering that movement happens on the exhalation.

> Through this process all of the limbs are differentiated and then reintegrated into an articulate whole-body pattern. Each body part will learn that it can initiate movement independently of the other parts, but is at the same time connected and related to them through the navel, affecting and responding to the whole. This process of differentiation and integration will be seen again at each level of development of movement and consciousness and is also basic to all methods of education and therapy, both physical and psychological. As we differentiate, we can dis-identify from the part, then reintegrate it at a new level of wholeness and awareness. This enables us to relate with a higher degree of consciousness and skill to the individual parts of ourselves and to the environment without losing the integrity of the whole.
> (Hartley, 1995:30)

After a few repetitions of the *Starfish Breathing* exercise the Developmental Movement Sequence can be taken as follows:

1) *Caterpillar* (the spinal push developmental pattern):

> The spinal push...can be recognized in the young infant's ability to wriggle itself to the far end of its crib before any controlled motor ability has developed in its arms and legs to assist this movement. The infant ["caterpillars"] by alternately flexing and extending its whole spine, pushing the body gradually along...
> (Hartley, 1995:52)

2) *Frog* and D*onkey* (the homolateral reach and pull pattern).

Leaping like a frog involves starting in a crouched position and then reaching forward with both arms simultaneously. Then the legs 'jump' to the new position of the hands. Kicking like a donkey is the reverse. Starting in the same crouched position, the legs 'kick' up and back simultaneously away from the hands and then the hands are brought back to the new position of the feet.

> The homolateral reach and pull patterns express the mind of "outer intention," and courage, commitment and trust. This is where we first learn to leap wholeheartedly into the unknown territory beyond the safety of our personal space. (ibid:76)

3) *Lizard* (the homolateral push pattern):

> As the opposite leg flexes in, it prepares to push; the impulse from the foot pushing against the floor travels upward along the spine and through the arm on the same side. The leg, torso and arm of this side are now fully elongated and bearing the weight, while the opposite side flexes in preparation for another push from the foot and foreleg of this side. (ibid:77)

Lizard

29

4) *Cat* (crawling - the contralateral reach and pull pattern). Try crawling backwards too!

> A sequential rotation through the spine underlies the action of the Contralateral patterns and creates the possibility for movement through all planes simultaneously. Such movement is a spiralling and allows for the continuous transitioning between levels and directions. The Contralateral pattern has a distinctly different rhythm from the Homolateral, much lighter and often more swift and fluid. It may express the quality of a wild cat stalking its prey, alert and sensitive. (ibid:79-80)

Cat - the contralateral reach and pull pattern

5) *Bear* (further Contralateral patterning work)

In moving like a bear the knees are lifted from the ground and all the support is found alternating between the hands and feet. It is important to stress here that adults and children are encouraged to open the full palms of the hands to the floor and to be articulate in working through the soles of the feet. After working through this developmental patterning 'warm-up' (and believe me you will be warm!) it is nice to come up to standing – taking the spine to vertical after being a starfish, lizard, frog, donkey, cat and bear! You may wish to simply walk around the space with your child (also a Contralateral patterning movement) for a bit.

Bear - Contralateral work

After walking, stop and rest back on the mat with your child. Now may be a nice time to briefly experiment with your child demonstrating to each other how your child's imagination can influence their physicality. This brief exercise called 'Rock/Feather' is a good preparation for the FLY section of the Big Dog Little Dog practice.

Stand facing your child and have them imagine that they are a rock, heavy, solid, dense, dark…tell them to maintain that image as you try to lift them.

Lifting the 'rock' – note Lincoln's flexed feet, arms in towards his midline to make himself more compact and his cheeky grin (as he knows it will be a challenge for me to lift him!)

Lifting a 'feather' is much easier! Note Lincoln's relaxed feet, open fingers and how much higher I am able to physically lift him.

In this simple image based exercise where the child discovers how they can help you lift them in the FLY work. It is also a nice illustration of how to work with our body-mind -- a unity that we so often forget.

FLY

There are always two and sometimes four people involved in a 'flying' pose in the Big Dog Little Dog class. 'The Flyer' (the child) and 'The Base' (the adult) are always involved in the pose. On occasion, another child/adult pair joins them when "spotters" are needed. Spotters are needed in asymmetrical poses where balance is challenged for the 'base' or when points of contact between the 'base' and flyer' are reduced from four to two (like in *High Chair* pose). Working at home however you may not have this "spotter" option available to you. In this case, work on building your confidence and skill with the symmetrical poses first. Remember to practice in areas that are clear of "stuff" (no toys or clutter) and if you feel like folded blankets around you may make a safer, softer environment then feel free to set these up before you FLY too.

PREPARING TO FLY

It is a good idea to start new 'flyers' (your child) with a simple exercise of giving weight to their 'base' (you) whilst remaining on the ground. This is useful for nervous 'flyers' or 'bases'. I call this exercise the L*eg Press.*

Lie on your back and place your feet in a turned out position just below your child's hip bones (or where feels comfortable for the 'flyer').

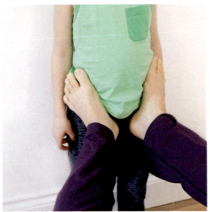

In the L*eg Press* exercise the 'flyer' keeps their body strong and straight; I usually say "like a board" so that the 'base' (you) can simply flex and extend your knees to push the 'flyer' away and bring them back. If your child has difficulty in keeping their body strong and straight then often you can have them do *plank* (or *double plank* with you - see page 21) so that they can feel the work needed in their body to keep their body strong.

Leg Press

Leg Press establishes the initial eye contact, trust and weight distribution needed in all the other flying poses to come. Once you feel that you and your child have the hang of the *Leg Press*, a smooth transition into your *Forward Fly Preparation* is just to take your child's hands as shown in the photograph - with the "flyers fingers front".

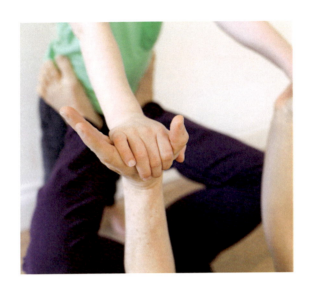

Forward Fly Preparation

Then all that needs to happen is for your child to extend their arms and legs and lift their chest. Together you find the point of balance.

Forward Fly

With practice and as the child's strength grows you may be able to release hands!

Forward Fly without support

Transition into the next pose *Deep Fold* from here by simply having your child fold forward from their hips into your legs. *Deep Fold* is a lovely therapeutic pose for the 'flyer' as it gently tractions the spine. The 'flyer' should maintain a little bit of effort in their legs (it helps to have the 'flyer's legs wide and backwards) to balance the weight of their torso coming downward.

Deep Fold

From *Deep Fold* your child can move their hands up to their face and hold their own chin to find *The Thinker*. Help them to support the weight of their head by holding and lifting their elbows. This will give your child a lovely backbend through their spine.

The Thinker

Hedgehog is another pose which is possible to access from the basic *Forward Fly* position. It involves your child bending their knees and bringing the soles of their feet together. Your child can then reach through your legs to grab hold of their own feet or ankles. If they have difficulty finding this position, have them come down and try it as a seated pose on the floor.

Hedgehog

If your child is comfortable in *Hedgehog* and feels they can hold it for some time then it may be advantageous to try *Revolving Hedgehog*. This is where the whole shape is held and turned 180 degrees so that the child ends up with their spine touching your legs.

Revolving Hedgehog Preparation: Get ready to transfer the child's weight from both of your feet into your opposite hand and foot. In order to do this, take your child's shoulder (as shown in this case with the 'base's' left hand) and support your child's spine with your other hand (as shown in this case with the right hand).

Revolving Hedgehog Preparation

The photo below shows the first part of the rotation whereby your foot (in this case the right foot) is replaced with your hand (the right hand which was on their spine a moment ago). As in the preparation, you will need to keep stabilizing the child with your other hand on their shoulder.

In bringing your child around, replace your hand with your foot again (in this case right hand for the right foot). You can use the right hand on the child's knee to continue to guide them around as you slot your feet into the folds of your child's hips.

...and we're around! A happy *Revolving Hedgehog.*

There is a fun way to dismount after *Revolving Hedgehog* and it is called the *Kick-over Dismount.* It works like this: your child releases from the *Hedgehog* position and you stabilize your child's torso with your arms as your child holds your arms for extra support. When your child feels ready they "kick-over" reaching their legs to the ground as you help to guide them there. Wait until they are solid on their feet until releasing the support from their torso.

If your child is a keen 'flyer' then from the *Kick-over Dismount* they may be ready to go up again. An easy transition is to have them turn 180 degrees so that they are still standing at your head, but they have turned from their "landing" to face away from you. This sets them up nicely for *Angel*.

Angel is a backbend where your feet support your child's upper back whilst holding your child's ankles to provide a gentle traction through their spine. *Angel* is a pose I introduce once there is a great deal of trust that has been established between adult and child; particularly in the *Backward Fly*. In this manual I have chosen to describe *Angel* before describing *Backward Fly* as it works well in terms to sequencing to follow on from the *Kick-over Dismount*. Just to be aware though that I consider *Angel* to be more advanced than the *Backward Fly* position (which is described on the following pages).

Overhead Mount

The child needs to initiate the preparation for *Angel* and they do this by lifting through their chest and "dropping back" into the 'base's' awaiting feet. This is called the *Overhead Mount*. Your feet should be close together so that your child feels that they have a supportive platform on which to rest their upper spine. In the beginning, your child may wish to take hold of your ankles as they guide themselves into this backbend.

*Angel
Drop-backs*

It is worth noting that a useful preparation for *Forward Fly* was to practice *plank* and *double plank*. Likewise, in preparation for *Hedgehog* it is useful for students to practice baddha konasana (soles of feet together, knees bent) seated on the floor. Here, in the process of learning *Angel*, a useful preparation exercise would be to practice "drop-backs" with your child. "Drop-backs" are found in Ashtanga Yoga and are, in early stages, practiced with an assist. You can assist your child by having them "drop-back" to the floor and come up again with your support.

As they "drop-back" the head leads and the rest of the spine follows. As they come up the heart (chest) leads the movement and the spine follows. A short video of this can be viewed here: https://www.youtube.com/watch?v=YQar1KeuY6k

If the child is confident in *Angel* and the mechanics of "drop-backs" then a fun way to evolve *Angel* pose is to replicate the "drop-backs" in the air! I call them *Angel Drop-backs* (photos of this are on the previous page). The child stays relaxed in their backbend while you lever them forward and back; bringing their hands to touch the floor and then lifting them back over so their feet touch the floor. This can be repeated as many times as you both enjoy doing it.

Just as the basic *Forward Fly* position is the basis for *Deep Fold*, *The Thinker* and *Hedgehog*. There now come a series of flying poses that originate from the basic *Backward Fly* position and these are called *Reverse Bow*, *Rag Doll* and *The Hanger*.

First, there is the basic *Backward Fly*. This is set up with your feet positioned at the gluteal fold (base of their buttocks) and your hands over their shoulders. For further stability, your child can reach back and hold your shins.

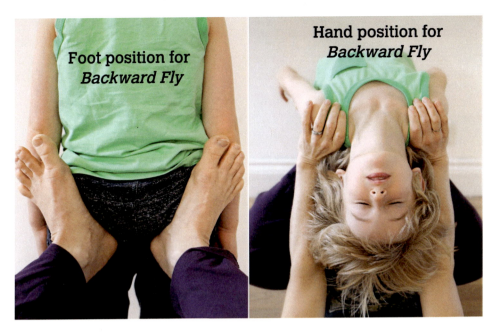

The child needs to lift their chest (as in back-drops) and lean back into the support of your hands as you extend your legs to lift them up.

Reverse Bow

Reverse Bow is a transition for the 'flyer'. From the *Backward Fly* position the 'flyer' reaches toward their feet, bends their knees and takes hold of their ankles.

Rag Doll

Rag Doll is a combined effort from both you and your child. From the *Reverse Bow* position, your child releases their ankles yet keeps the knees bent. As they do this, move your hands one at a time from their shoulders to their upper (thoracic) spine. In this way your hands act as a supportive platform for their upper spine just like your feet did in *Angel*. Once you are in the *Rag Doll* position, begin to 'pedal' your legs (like riding a bicycle) to encourage a release through your child's hips. This can feel freeing and fun if done with a sense of ease.

Another pose to be accessed from the basic *Backward Fly* position is *The Hanger*. *The Hanger* is a full inversion and provides a lovely traction for your child's whole spine.

The Hanger

From the basic *Backward Fly* position your child will need to change the angle of their pelvis. In the *Backward Fly* position their hip joint is in extension. In *The Hanger*, their hip joint is in flexion. Working together, as your child changes the angle of their pelvis, bring your feet around to support their thighs. This is a small change for both of you and if done with control and awareness should be an easy transition.

From any of the backward flying positions, the *Cuddle Dismount* can be taken. Gently guide your child down onto your body (you will mainly control this through strength in your arms but you both should be in communication about what is happening).

Stay as long as you like here – enjoying a cuddle.

The next pose: *High Chair*, introduces a new mount, called the *Stirrup Mount*.

Stirrup Mount

The *Stirrup Mount* is set up first of all with your child standing with one foot either side of your torso. Have your child then sit back onto your bent knees. Once they are seated, make stirrups with your hands (elbows on the floor and wrists over elbows) that your child can step into.

High Chair pose, done without a spotter, is a real test of core strength for your child and it may be that much practice is needed before your child can access *High Chair* without the assistance of a spotter.

Once your child's feet are grounded in the stirrups, they can then take their weight forwards, using their own hands against your legs to help them "push-off" and go up to standing in the stirrups. As this happens, be ready to extend your own legs and make a seat with your feet for your child.

High Chair
from *Stirrup Mount*

When your child feels balanced in their *High Chair*, they can take their arms up for even more height.

SUPPORT

The support section involves the following inversions (unless there are contraindications): *Headstand* (or rabbit variation), *Handstand* and *Shoulderstand*. All of these inversions are done with the support of the wall and/or the support of each other.

There are two approaches to *Headstand* that are taught in the Big Dog Little Dog classes and they are: the triangle base (as illustrated in this photo), and the rabbit base (as taught in the Ashtanga yoga primary series where the back of the skull is cradled in interwoven hands).

There are two ways to come into *Handstand* using the wall. The first, and easiest, is to start in down dog with the heels against the wall. Then you simply "walk" your legs up the wall. If you keep the legs parallel to the floor then you can work your alignment into a 'truer' sensation of an unsupported *Handstand*.

The second, and more dynamic way to access *Handstand* is to set the hands shoulder width apart near (but not touching) the wall and "kick" the legs up. This is for stronger students who would like to try to use the wall merely as a 'crutch' as they attempt a balance without touching the wall.

Lincoln and Grace have walked their legs up the wall into *Handstand* from a downward dog position.

This photograph of *Shoulderstand* is shown without the support of the wall but when taught in the Big Dog Little Dog classes it is introduced with support. To set up using the wall, begin sitting side-on to the wall and then swing your legs up the wall, feet pointing towards the ceiling. Then bend your knees and press your feet into the wall thereby lifting the pelvis without much effort. Support your back with both hands, feeling an equal relationship of your back resting in hands and your hands pushing into your back.

Inversions build confidence and strength. Inversions also feed into the child's ability to be comfortable seeing the world upside down; which they do a lot of in the FLY section. Children also enjoy seeing their parents working hard at inverting their body and often children find it easier to invert than adults. This brings them a sense of empowerment as they encourage their parents/carers: "If I can do it so can you!"

CALM

After the heated work of inversions it is time to cool and calm the body. Some final stretches and some softer connections bring us eventually back to the breath in relaxation. There are a few different ways presented here in terms of calming and connecting in this section: *Leg Love*, *The Washing Machine*, *The Kissing Twist* and *Soft Folds*.

Leg Love

Leg Love (a term coined by Acroyoga) is used to release tension in the back and hips of the 'base' after flying work. It is, in essence an intuitive metamorphosis of leg mobilizing that is guided by your child. Lie on your back and have your child move your legs in circles (or one leg at a time if the child is small). They can pull your legs away from your body providing a gentle traction to the spine. This feels great (if you can get the child to focus on it for more than 30 seconds!)

The Washing Machine

The Washing Machine is set up facing each other and your legs spread wide. Have your child place their feet on the inside of your legs. Then, working together, circle the top half of your body (your torso) over the bottom half (your pelvis). Kids like to go a bit crazy on this one… the equivalent of a washing machine on its fastest spin cycle. So I say something like: "Now, we're going to set this washing machine to its 'delicates' cycle and on the slowest spin." That's why this is part of the CALM section.

The *Kissing Twist* is one of my favourite postures in the whole of the Big Dog Little Dog practice and it was one of the first poses that my children and I developed. We took the Yin yoga pose *Twisted Root* which is a reclining twist and added kisses! In the pose, the legs and hips are anchoring, the spine is lengthening, and the opposite shoulder blade (to the direction of the legs) is reaching for the floor. The child kisses from the head of the shoulder joint all the way to the wrist. Some children prefer to 'walk' their fingers down from the shoulder to the wrist. Either is fine and the sensations from your child's kisses or touch will encourage your arm and shoulder to drop towards the floor, further grounding the shoulder girdle in the pose. Done with sincerity, it is lovely and calm for both of you.

The Kissing Twist

For this final pose in the CALM section, most children will need to sit on a block so that they can align their spine against the spine of their parent or carer more easily. In the set up for these *Soft Folds,* both you and your child sit back to back. Sit for a moment, feeling for each others' breath through the back of your bodies. Feel movement in the back of the lungs as the air is drawn in and expelled. Feel each other's weight equally, leaning into each other and also supporting each other simultaneously. Then, keeping your spines connected, slowly fold forward, let your child follow, like lying back in an easy chair. After a few breaths, initiate movement to come back up and push with your hands against the floor to bring your child back up to upright. Then, let your child softly fold. You will need to place your hands behind you as you go back so that you do not make your child bear your full weight. This gentle backward/forward motion of *Soft Folds* can take place as many times as you both like. Your legs can be in any comfortable position: straight in front, stretched out wide (like in *The Washing Machine*) or crossed (if crossing, change the leg that is in front for the second forward fold).

Soft Folds

REST

Finally, we take rest. In yoga asana (posture based) traditions, this is the pose of great reward and often regarded as the most important pose of an asana practice. The body is stilled, the mind is quieted and the breath becomes the focus. This pose called *savasana*, is a chance for child to shift their attention to the comfort and well-being of their parent/carer (even if just for a moment).

When it is time to take rest, ask your child if they would like to gather two blankets and an eye pillow (if you have one) for you. Then, they "tuck" you in. This is a wonderful thing to witness as a Big Dog Little Dog teacher: children placing a blanket under their parent/carer's head, covering them with the other blanket and then gently placing an eye pillow over their eyes. It is a lovely chance for a role reversal and in my experience, children love doing it.

Once you are "tucked-in" let your child choose how they would like to be in relationship to you. I always give options (they may wish for an extra blanket for themselves): they can lie on top of your body, they can lie beside you, they can lie head to head with you, with your ears touching and then reaching up to cup each other's opposite ear. These are times of surrender; surrendering to breath, to gravity, to each other.

After REST (taking as long a rest as you both like), gently rise back up through to sitting. To close the practice, face each other or your child can sit in your lap. In these last moments, both of you could bring your hands together in front of your hearts, and follow your own breath to lift your chest as you inhale and as you exhale then release the weight of the head forward toward your hands. Maybe you would feel it appropriate to say "thank you" to each other or "I love you". This is an opportunity to observe the strength of your bond and notice any increase in trust and connection.

About the author:

April is mother to Lincoln (age 7) and Grace (age 5) who have both helped her to develop the Big Dog Little Dog content. April's career has always had an educational focus. Prior to founding Big Dog Little Dog, April was a Lecturer in Dance in UK universities and in her early career she worked as a primary school teacher in the US. She has a PhD in dance with an expertise in human movement analysis and has been teaching yoga for over 20 years in the styles of Ashtanga and Yin yoga.

Bibliography

Baba Hari Dass (1981). *Ashtanga Yoga Primer.* Santa Cruz, California: Sri Rama Publishing

Black, J. & Puckett, M. (2005). *The Young Child: Development from Prebirth through Age Eight.* New Jersey: Pearson

Hartley, L. (1995). *Wisdom of the Body Moving.* Berkley, California: North Atlantic Books

Juhan, D. (2003). *Job's Body: A Handbook for Bodywork.* New York: Station Hill Press

Levine, S. (1997). *A Year to Live.* New York: Bell Tower Publishing

Olsen, A. (1998). *BodyStories: A Guide to Experiential Anatomy.* New Hampshire: University Press of New England

Rosenberg, L. (1998). *Breath by Breath.* Boston: Shambhala Publications

Scott, J. (2000). *Ashtanga Yoga.* London: Gaia Books

Lightning Source UK Ltd.
Milton Keynes UK
UKRC031902221122
412680UK00005B/119